First published by Scholastic Australia Pty Limited in 2023.

ISBN 978-1-339-00860-8

10 9 8 7 6 5 4 3 2 1   23 24 25 26 27

Printed in the U.S.A.   37

This edition first printing, August 2023

Cover design by Hannah Janzen and Ashley Vargas

Internal design by Paul Hallam

Typeset in Dawet Ayu, Silkscreen, LOGX-10, Apercu Mono, and Ate Bit

MONDAY MORNING

"Aaaand this part of the volcano," Mr. Rockface droned, "is called . . . anyone?"

My eyes drooped.

Heavy eyelids.

Sleep so close . . .

"ARI AVATAR?" Mr. Rockface said.

My head whipped up to attention.

"Er . . . ah . . . um, could you repeat . . ." I mumbled as I saw a frown form on Mr. Rockface's block face.

Jez **COUGHED** loudly. Cough, "Magma chamber," cough, cough.

"Magma chamber?" I ventured.

"Correct," Mr. Rockface said, his frown disappearing.

I turned to Jez, one of my best friends, who was sitting to my right, and mouthed, "Thanks, bruh." She'd just saved my **BLOCKY BUTT.**

"Only Mr. Rockface could make something as cool as volcanoes this boring," my other best friend, Zeke, whispered to me from his seat to my left.

I nodded. He was totally right.

DING, DING, DING!

Finally!

"Before you go, avatars, I have some exciting news," Mr. Rockface said in a flat voice. He even made exciting announcements sound boring. "This Wednesday, we are going on a **FIELD TRIP.**"

I sat up straighter. That sounded cool. Going on a field trip was usually more fun than sitting in a classroom.

"We are going to Mount Blockus

to see our volcano studies in action," he said.

Wait, **WHAT?!**

The class erupted into cheers of delight, high fives, and fist bumps.

"A VOLCANO?!" Zeke shrieked. "IRL?!"

"Hang on, hang on," a little voice said from the front of the room.

The whole class **GROANED.**

"Yes, **GABE?"** Mr. Rockface

said, rolling his eyes. Even the teacher was annoyed by Gabe.

Gabe was the **NERDIEST** avatar ever. He was, like, two years younger than us but was in our grade because he's a brainiac.

But that's not what was annoying about him. The annoying part was that he was obsessed with safety. Like that time we went on a field trip to the waterslide park for Math class. We were supposed to time how long it took to get from the top of the slide to the bottom. But Gabe pointed out to the teachers that we hadn't done a proper "risk assessment plan" (whatever that meant!) and so we shouldn't be allowed to actually go on the waterslides. The teachers agreed and we spent the entire field trip watching other avatars have an awesome time.

LAME!

"Have you properly assessed the

risks of this field trip, as well as completed a thorough report on the dangers we may encounter?" Gabe asked.

"Yes, Gabe," Mr. Rockface said. "This volcano is classified as **EXTINCT,** which means the risks are minimal."

"What's that mean?" I asked.

Mr. Rockface rolled his eyes again. "Ari, if you had been listening to the lesson you would know that 'dormant' means it may erupt again, but 'extinct' means it won't."

Everyone slumped down, deflated, except for Gabe, who looked happy with the news.

"So, it's just, like, a mountain? No lava?" someone from the back of the classroom said.

"That's right. But there will be a lot of interesting rocks to look at," Mr. Rockface said.

UGH!

"YAY!" cheered Gabe.

"Permission slips have been emailed

to your parents and I would like you to remind them to fill in the form before the field trip."

Me and my whole class packed up our books and trudged out the door, disappointed that our volcano field trip was now just a walk around a mountain, picking up rocks.

BOOORRRIIIIIING!

We walked through the school toward our lockers.

"Our Geography field trip sounds cool," Jez said to Zeke and me, stacking her books into her locker.

Jez was, like, the smartest avatar I'd ever met. If anyone was going to get excited about analyzing rocks, it would be her. Not as excited as she might be over **HACKING** into a top secret computer system, but a close second. Even though she was a total tech whiz, she wasn't an annoying **NERD** like Gabe, thank goodness.

"Jez, it's *rocks*," Zeke whined.

"Some of those rocks would have

been part of a massive volcanic **ERUPTION** thousands of years ago. Looking at them is like traveling back in time!" she said with wide eyes.

Zeke and I exchanged looks.

"Time travel?" Zeke said, shaking his head. "A—Completely impossible, and B—nowhere near as cool."

"Well, we may not be able to see lava IRL, but it's given me an idea," Jez said. "Who's free this afternoon for some **THE FLOOR IS LAVA** time?"

My eyes lit up. *The Floor Is Lava* was one of our favorite games to play at Zeke's house. Zeke had the coolest house because his dad was an **OBBY** designer and he always had prototypes in his backyard. The idea of the game was that you had to get from one place to another without touching the ground.

"What do you think?" I asked Zeke hopefully.

"Yeah, I'm free, sounds awesome!" he said, putting his hands up to high-five us both. "And we can even tell my parents that it's homework because it's a game about lava!"

We all **LAUGHED.**

It was going to be **EPIC!**

MONDAY AFTERNOON

"Aw man, it's **RAINING!**" I said, peering out the window into Zeke's yard.

Thick droplets of rain were **POUNDING** against the window of Zeke's living room.

"Maybe we should just do some gaming instead," Zeke said, sounding deflated.

"Hang on," Jez said, sitting up

straighter. "Why don't we just play it inside?"

"EPIC!" Zeke and I yelled in unison.

Zeke's living room joined to the dining area, which then joined to his kitchen through a doorway.

"OK, everyone has to get to the kitchen counter. We've got seven minutes to complete the course," Zeke said, setting his watch. "And remember . . ."

"THE FLOOR IS LAVA!" we all screamed.

I stood up on the couch and
looked around. Zeke gave me
a grin, then did a massive jump
over the coffee table to the couch
on the other side of the room.

"Nailed it!" he whooped.

I knew I couldn't jump that far—
Zeke was a **PARKOUR
PRO.** So I threw some of the
cushions onto the ground to make
a line of stepping stones over to
the coffee table. I **LEAPED** from
one to the other, **WOBBLING** on
my landings but making sure
I didn't touch the floor.

Jez went a different way,
swiveling the armchair around,
then climbing onto the piano stool.

I jumped from the last cushion to
the coffee table but then realized
I was **TRAPPED.**

At this point, Zeke was already leaping to the chair in the dining room, then climbing onto the table.

"Bruh—I'm **STUCK!**" I yelled, looking around.

Zeke **WHIPPED** his head from side to side with a frown, trying to find a solution.

"I've got you!" Jez said from the piano stool.

Next to her was a **BROOM.** She threw it to me and I was able to use it to make a path from the coffee table over to the first dining chair. I **TIPTOED** across the broom handle, balancing as carefully as possible to avoid falling to the floor.

"Made it!" I hooted.

Jez then took a **MASSIVE LEAP** and landed on her butt in the middle of a beanbag. She then dove across to the dining table, so all three of us were standing on it.

"FIVE MINUTES to go," Zeke said, checking his watch.

The doorway into the kitchen was too far to jump through, even for Zeke. We looked around quickly.

"THERE!" I said, pointing to a basket of clean laundry on the end of the dining table.

Zeke gently tossed the whole basket forward, toward the kitchen doorway. With a soft jump, he **LANDED** inside the basket in a crouch. The basket wobbled slightly, and Jez and I winced, thinking Zeke might fall over. But he regained his balance and gave us a thumbs-up.

From there, Zeke jumped upward and grabbed onto the doorframe, hanging by his fingertips.

"Whoa, bruh!" I was impressed.

He then did a chin-up and kicked his legs forward into a **SWING.** He released his hands and flew through the doorway and onto the kitchen counter.

"EPIC!" Jez cheered.

Jez and I both knew we weren't pro enough to pull off that kind of trick.

"How do we get across?" Jez
asked Zeke.

Zeke assessed the space, then
his face lit up. There was a pile
of place mats next to him, and he
FRISBEED them through the
doorway so they acted like blocks
in an obby course.

Jez and I jumped from one
place mat to the other like
stepping stones, leaping
toward the kitchen counter.

The last jump was going to be
the biggest and hardest.

Jez was in front, so she went first. She leaped and Zeke stretched out his arm to catch her. Their fingertips touched, but Jez fell backward onto the cold floor.

"AAAAH!" she squealed. "The lava!!" She pretended to melt into a pit of lava.

"NOOOOOOOOOO!" Zeke and I fake-screamed, imagining Jez sinking into the molten liquid.

"You're our last chance," Zeke told me.

I **JUMPED** as far as I could and Zeke grabbed my arm in midair. He hoisted me up onto the counter and I stood **TRIUMPHANTLY.**

"Made it!" I gave him a fist bump.

"But we lost a friend in the process," Zeke said, looking down at the floor where Jez lay, pretending to have **MELTED.**

"What on **EARTH** is going on?!" an angry voice shouted.

UH-OH.

Zeke's mom was standing in the doorway. She had her hands on her hips and a big frown on her block face.

We stared at the **CHAOS** we'd caused—footprints on the kitchen counter, place mats splayed through the doorway, cushions all around the floor, and there were dirty marks on the clean laundry, which had been smooshed flat inside the basket. There were even some grubby fingerprints on the top of the doorway where Zeke had done his chin-up.

"Oh, sorry, Mom!" Zeke said, jumping down from the counter. He reached a hand out to Jez, helping her to her feet.

"Yeah, sorry!" I added, following him and grabbing a cloth to wipe the footprints off the counter.

"You avatars better clean this mess up **RIGHT QUICK!**" she said.

"Yes, we will," we chorused.

We all watched as Zeke's mom left, waiting a few seconds before turning to each other. A smile crept across Zeke's face. "That was **PRO!**"

Then we all burst out laughing.

TUESDAY LUNCHTIME

Jez, Zeke, and I lined up in the cafeteria, waiting to get our food. I slid my plastic tray along the top of the counter. Behind the glass divider were angry-looking avatars serving the food, **SLOPPING** it onto the plates of bored-looking avatar kids.

The avatar behind the counter dumped some **CHICKEN NUGGETS** onto my plate. I shuffled my tray along to

the next avatar and he put
a spoonful of vegetables next to
the chicken. They were a weird
color and looked kind of frozen.
I chose a drink and then carried
my tray outside into the sunshine.

Zeke, Jez, and I scanned the
playground for a vacant table,
but all of them were full. Well, all
except for the one **GABE** was
sitting at, inspecting his nuggets.

"We could sit there?" Jez said,
gesturing toward Gabe.

"No, not Gabe," I protested. "He'll

lecture us about the chances of us choking on our lunch."

Gabe looked up and saw us. His eyes **WIDENED** in hope as he smiled at us.

UUUUUUGH!

I glanced at Zeke and Jez and could tell they were both thinking the same thing.

"Oh alright, then," I huffed.

"Hey, Gabe, wassup?" Zeke said, sliding in next to him.

"The **SKY** is up!" Gabe said, laughing loudly at his own joke.

CRINGE.

I picked up a nugget and lifted it to my mouth.

"WAIT!" Gabe yelled, startling me into dropping my nugget onto the floor. He reached into his backpack and pulled out a little thermometer. Then he shuffled over to me and **STUCK IT** right inside one of the nuggets on my plate.

"What are you doing?!" I asked.

"I'm checking that your chicken was cooked to the correct temperature. If it wasn't, then you risk salmonella **FOOD POISONING!**" Gabe said. He pulled the thermometer out and squinted at it. "All good, carry on."

Jez and Zeke laughed.

"Dude, why are you, like, so **OBSESSED** with safety and stuff?" I asked.

Gabe tilted his head to the side. "It's better to be **SAFE** than sorry, right?"

"Well, yeah, but how are you meant to have any **FUN** if you're always worrying about things going wrong?" Zeke asked.

Gabe frowned, thinking. It was like he'd never contemplated that before. "My mom is a risk assessor."

"A what?" Zeke asked.

"A risk assessor. Her whole job is working out how dangerous something is and whether it's worth the risk. Most of the time, she doesn't like me **TAKING RISKS** because she says the risk of harm is worse than the fun I might have."

Gabe looked down. He seemed a little sad. I couldn't help but feel a bit sorry for him.

Gabe reached into his bag and pulled out a **NOTEBOOK** and pencil. He started scribbling some things down in a table he had drawn. Gabe was always pulling that thing out and writing stuff.

"What have we got here?" a snide voice said from behind us.

We turned and saw **TRIP,** the school bully, standing with his two blockhead friends, Levi and Elle, on either side of him.

"Get lost, Trip," Jez said, irritated.

Trip spent entire lunch breaks walking around the school, searching for avatars to tease or aggravate.

"Got a **NEW FRIEND** here?" he jeered, poking Gabe in the back.

"Leave him alone," I said, standing up. Gabe might be annoying sometimes, but he didn't deserve to be picked on.

"Why? Is he your new BFF, Ari Avatar?" Trip taunted.

Elle and Levi snickered.

"What are you writing in your little book?" Trip said, **POKING** Gabe again. "Let me guess. You're figuring out the risk of sitting on the ground. Who knows? There might be an earthquake! Or an ant might bite you on the butt!"

"GO AWAY, Trip," Jez said.

Trip sneered at her, then reached forward and **SNATCHED** Gabe's notebook from his hands.

"Hey!" Gabe protested. "That's mine! Give it back!"

Trip **DANGLED** it over Gabe's head, just out of reach, as Gabe tried to jump and get his notebook.

"Give it back!" I yelled, feeling my block face color with **ANGER.**

"You gonna make me?" Trip laughed.

I lunged forward, but Trip threw the notebook to Levi, who caught it. "Go long, Trip!" he said.

Trip **RACED** down the hill, getting ready for Levi to fling Gabe's notebook down to him.

Gabe's eyes were filling with tears.

REEEEEE!

I jumped up off my seat and picked up my **LUNCH TRAY.** I dumped my food out onto the table and raced over to the top of the hill. Trip was sprinting down and I'd never catch him by running.

So I took a massive run-up and then leaped onto my plastic food tray. I **SURFED** the tray down the grassy hill, gaining speed as I went. It was much quicker than running, and I could feel the wind whipping through my hair as I went faster and faster.

I glanced behind me and saw Levi hurl the notebook down the hill toward Trip. Trip turned to receive the pass but noticed I was gaining on him.

"No, you don't!" he hollered, leaping into the air to catch the notebook.

As I **ZOOMED** toward him, I stuck out my foot to the side and **TRIPPED** him. Yeah, *trip* on that, Trip!

TRIP!

The notebook flew out of his hands and into the air. I ducked down low to go even faster, then launched myself off the tray and into the air, **CATCHING** the notebook mid-flight.

"I'LL GET YOU, ARI!"

Trip threatened furiously from

where he had landed in the dirt.

I walked back up the hill with the tray under my arm and Gabe's notebook in my hand.

"WHOA, that was epic," Gabe said with a smile.

"NO SWEAT," I said, patting him on the back and handing him the notebook.

"Looks like I owe you one!" he said.

I smiled lightly. He was a good kid. But there was **NO WAY** that little avatar was ever going to be a help to me. But that's OK. I was happy to do him a favor, even though he'd never be able to give me anything in return.

TUESDAY NIGHT

I could smell the **LASAGNA** coming out of the oven as I hopped down the stairs toward the dining table.

"Ari, please pour some water for everyone," Dad said. "Ally, set the table."

My annoying sister, Ally, gathered up a handful of silverware and started laying it out on the table. Mom walked in and sniffed the air.

"Ooh, smells good, chef!" She kissed my dad on the cheek.

GROSS!!!!!!!

Dad brought out the steaming lasagna and put it in the middle of the table on a place mat. He started to cut it up and dish out portions onto each plate.

"So, field trip tomorrow, Ari?" he said as he plopped a slice on my plate.

"Yeah, but I think it's going to be **BORING.**"

"Why's that?" Mom asked. "You're going to a volcano! I thought you would have been thrilled!"

"It's one of those **EXTINCT** volcanoes. It doesn't even have lava. We're just looking at rocks on the ground," I mumbled as I scooped some food into my mouth.

NOM, NOM, NOM!

"And that kid Gabe is in my class. He always makes sure we never do anything fun because he thinks it's too **'RISKY,'** then the teachers agree and we end up doing nothing. Like that time we went to a **CANDY FACTORY** and he wasn't convinced the machinery hadn't come into contact with any allergens, so we didn't get to eat anything in case someone was allergic. But all the other avatars from the other schools on the same field trip were allowed to eat as much free candy as they liked. So **UNFAIR!"**

Dad hid a smile behind his hand.

"Well, maybe it wouldn't hurt to be a little more prepared in life," Mom said, defending Gabe as usual. "Do you want to remind me why your clothes upstairs are all wet?"

"Oh, sure, I **FORGOT** my umbrella and it ended up raining in the afternoon. But it wasn't my fault! It was a sunny day this morning!" I protested.

"I'm sure Gabe had an umbrella," Ally teased. "He probably had two."

"Who asked you?" I said, irritated.

"Ari, be nice," Dad warned. Ally stuck her tongue out at me when

Mom and Dad weren't looking.
I stuck my tongue out back at her.

We finished our dinner, and
I helped clear the plates and
stack the dishwasher. Then
I **RACED** back up to my room.
I knew I only had a few more
minutes left of screen time, and
I wanted to message Zeke.

Ari: You there, bruh?

Zeke: Yup. How fun was
that last game? We totally
bloxxed those noobs!

Ari: Epic!

Zeke: I gotta go but I'll c u tomorrow at the field trip.

Ari: Let's hope it's not totally BORING.

Zeke: It's an extinct volcano. Wat could even happen?

Ari: True. L8r!

WEDNESDAY MORNING

We stepped off **THE BOAT** and shielded our eyes from the bright sunlight. At least it was a nice day. There was nothing worse than a field trip in the rain. I peered up the **STEEP MOUNTAINSIDE** we would be climbing, all the way to the volcanic peak.

I had to admit, despite being extinct, the volcano actually looked pretty cool. It was basically its own island surrounded by a national park. We had to catch a small boat there from the mainland.

Mr. Rockface then droned on about all the rules of the field trip. **ZZZZZZZZZ.**

Instead of listening, Zeke and I started a thumb war. I totally **BLOXXED** Zeke, pinning his thumb down. He pulled back and we started giggling.

"Um, guys, I think you should be listening," a voice **HISSED** from next to us. *Gabe.* Always obsessing over the safety talk, as usual.

I rolled my eyes and went back to thumb wars with Zeke.

"Right, we need to form

GROUPS OF FOUR,"

Mr. Rockface said. "This will be your group for the day. You will act as one another's buddies so I'll know if anyone is missing at any point."

Jez, Zeke, and I immediately linked arms. We just needed to find one more person.

Some of our other avatar friends were already in groups. I didn't want Trip in our group, and he was already standing with Elle and Levi.

I looked around. Then I saw **GABE** sitting alone, staring down at his hands.

"Gabe, can you please join Trip's group?" Mr. Rockface said.

Gabe's eyes widened in horror. I knew there was no way he wanted to be in Trip's group.

"Actually, Gabe is in **OUR GROUP,**" I called out quickly.

Gabe's eyes lit up.

"What gives?" Zeke hissed.

"We can't leave him in Trip's group! He'll be **BULLIED** all day," I whispered.

Zeke knew I was right, and his face softened. "Come on, Gabe," he said, ushering him over to us.

"Now, we are all going to **HIKE** to the top of the volcano together.

When we get up there, break off into your groups and start walking around, making observations about your environment. You'll need to write this up in a presentation when you get back to school, so I advise you not to just mess around the whole time," Mr. Rockface said sternly. "There's a small information center near the top of the **VOLCANO.** It's run by the national park and has very interesting information about this volcano as well as other volcanoes. I recommend that you all go through the center and ask as many questions as you can to the national park ranger who works there."

"Will we have an **ADULT** avatar to guide us in our groups?" Gabe said, raising his hand.

The whole class **GROANED.** Even Mr. Rockface.

"No, Gabe. I will be there with all of the groups, and the area isn't big enough for anyone to get lost. If you stay with your groups within the area, you'll be fine," Mr. Rockface said.

"Gabe," Jez said evenly. "If you're going to hang out with us today, you're going to need to **CHILL OUT** just a bit, OK?"

"But . . ." Gabe started to protest. Then his shoulders relaxed when he saw Jez fold her arms. "OK."

We started our steep climb of the volcano. After a short while, things started to get a little **BORING.** Everything looked the same and I felt my breath laboring as we trudged up the mountainside.

"We need something to take our minds off the hike," Jez said, sensing my struggle.

"Let's play a game," Zeke said.

"How about *What Would You Do?*" I said. "Would you rather be stuck in an **ACID RAIN SHOWER** or swim across a **SHARK-INFESTED TANK?**"

"Sharks," Jez said. "I'm a good swimmer."

"Acid rain!" Zeke said. "I could

parkour my way through the drops and find shelter."

I thought about it. "I'm going with Zeke," I decided.

"Actually, it's dependent on a lot of variables," Gabe said, pulling out his **NOTEBOOK.** "How big is the shark tank? How many sharks? What breed of shark? What is the intensity of the acid rainstorm? What are the environmental factors that caused this weather anomaly?"

We all stared at Gabe.

"Ugh, forget about it," I said, annoyed. I didn't want to play anymore. Somehow, Gabe even managed to make a game a **TOTAL YAWN.** "Let's just keep walking."

It was going to be a *long* day.

WEDNESDAY LUNCHTIME

We finally made it to the peak of the volcano. I had to confess, it was kind of **WORTH IT** for the epic view from the top. We could see out over the national park, all the way across the sea, and could even see the city of Blockville on the horizon in the distance.

We formed our small groups and began walking around, taking notes about our surroundings.

Most of the ground was a dusty, ash color and there wasn't much growing there. We peered into the volcano, hoping to see a **LAKE OF LAVA** inside, but it was just a dried-up, empty hole.

We wandered over to a tiny building, which was the information center that Mr. Rockface had told us about. We went inside and it was pretty basic. There were posters on the wall with information about volcanoes and some rocks in glass cabinets.

A small, older avatar wearing the

national park uniform wandered
over to us.

"Hi, little avatars!" she said
jovially. "Want to learn more
about volcanoes?"

"YES!" Gabe cheered excitedly.

The little old avatar, whose
name tag read "Mildred," pointed
out different diagrams that showed
the layers of the volcano and all
the names of the various parts.

"Can this one **ERUPT?"** Zeke
asked, hoping for a bit of a thrill.

Mildred shook her head. "No, this one is extinct. Although they also thought Mount Bricknil was extinct, but one day . . . **KABOOM!**" She spread her hands out with a laugh.

I frowned nervously.

"What are these **METAL SHEETS?**" Jez asked, pointing to some squares hanging on the walls.

"These are a type of metal strong enough to withstand lava! This is what space shuttles are made from so they don't burn up while reentering the earth's atmosphere. Go on, you can touch it," Mildred urged.

We reached out and ran our hands along the smooth, cold metal trays.

"What would actually happen if the volcano *did* erupt?" Zeke asked.

"You'd want to get out of here quickly!" Mildred laughed. "And you'd need masks so you wouldn't breathe in the **TOXIC** fumes."

"I've got some—" Gabe began, but Zeke talked over the top of him.

"Could you **OUTRUN** a lava river?"

Mildred shook her head. "I don't think so!"

Mildred looked down. Her **WALKIE-TALKIE** started beeping and a scratchy voice came through the speaker.

"**YOU . . . MMZLESZZZZ . . . IMMEDIATELY . . . SHMZZZLE ZZZLE . . .**"

"I'm sorry, I can't hear you. Do you copy? You're breaking up," Mildred said into the speaker.

The walkie-talkie went silent.

"Oh dear. That was **BASE CAMP.** I'm not sure what is going on," she said as she pulled out her mobile phone. "And no reception, as usual. I'm sure it's nothing serious. I'll take the quad bike down and find out what's going on at base camp. But I might speak to your teacher about getting you kids back down too, just in case."

Mildred stepped out of the hut and into the open. She talked to Mr. Rockface, who nodded firmly, and then she pulled on a helmet and mounted her **QUAD BIKE.** With a roar, she started it up, then, to our surprise, launched into top gear. She bounced away on the bike, tearing down the mountainside.

"Who'd have guessed?" Jez said. "Mildred's a **DAREDEVIL!**"

We all laughed.

"Class, do your last rounds of looking around and taking notes. We are going to start our descent shortly," Mr. Rockface announced, clapping his hands.

"What? Why so soon?" Trip protested.

"The national park wants us to go back—it's not an emergency, just being cautious," he added.

Gabe looked nervous.

"Let's check out the **CRATER** again," Zeke said.

"Shouldn't we stay close to the class? We're leaving shortly," Gabe said.

"Mr. Rockface said we could have a final look around," I argued. "We've got time. Are you coming or not?"

"Well," Gabe said, thinking. "The teacher *did* say to stay with our groups."

"It's settled, then. Come on, Gabe,"
Jez said, following me and Zeke
back toward the volcano's crater.

The rest of the class had left the
center and was moving farther
down the mountain, so it was quiet
at the peak. I looked across the
expanse of the dried-up crater,
which used to be the mouth of
the volcano. But then something
caught my eye. Something tiny
was **GLISTENING** deep
inside the crater.

"What's that?" I said, pointing
down, deep into the gaping hole.

"What?" Zeke squinted.

I pointed toward a tiny crack that
was as thin as a strand of hair.
But the crack wasn't gray like
the rest of the volcano. It was a
bright, shining red.

"There," I said, pointing again.

"That looks like . . . like **LAVA!**"
Jez said with wide eyes.

"That's not possible," Gabe said,
coming over to the edge of the
opening. "This volcano is extinct.
There is no lava."

He squinted as he peered over the edge. Then his eyes became big saucers. The hairline crack seemed to be getting **BIGGER.** And red liquid began seeping out of it.

Suddenly, there was a low **RUMBLING** noise.

"Wh—what's that?" I asked anxiously.

The ground beneath us began to **TREMBLE.**

Then I noticed that Mr. Rockface

was hurriedly ushering our class down the side of the volcano.

"We've gotta get out of here!" Jez said.

We all nodded in agreement and turned to run back to our class.

But the ground started to **SHAKE** more violently. We all lost our balance and fell to the floor.

"Whoa, that was a big one," Zeke said, standing up. "Let's go!"

I stood up too, then turned to help Jez and check for Gabe.

"Uh . . . **WHERE'S GABE?"** I said, searching wildly around me. "He was here just a second ago."

We turned our heads from left to right. Then we heard it. A small, distant voice. And it was coming

from **INSIDE** the mouth of

the volcano.

WEDNESDAY—
A BIT LATER

"HEEEELP!" a small voice called.

We leaned over the edge
of the crater and saw Gabe,
HANGING by one arm from
a rock that was jutting out of
the side.

"GABE!" I screamed.

"Help me!" he pleaded.

Below him, I could see that the

crater was beginning to fill up with lava. The small crack was now a **GAPING HOLE** and lava bubbled out and spread around the bottom of it. As it slowly began to fill, a strange burning smell filled my nostrils.

"We'll get you!" Zeke **YELLED.**
He was frantic, trying to find
something to lower down to Gabe
to help him up. But there wasn't
a single item that could help.

"I can run back to Mr. Rockface!"
Jez said.

I squinted down the mountainside.
"I'm pretty sure Mr. Rockface and
our entire class are halfway to
the bottom by now."

"Didn't he even notice we were
gone?!" Zeke asked.

"We're all the same group and are one another's buddies. Nobody will notice until later," Jez said.

"The buddy system is deeply flawed," Gabe called up in a surprisingly matter-of-fact voice.

The ground **SHOOK** again and the bubbling lava flowed faster, filling up the crater and inching toward Gabe's feet.

"HEEEELP!" he screamed again.

"There's no time. **AVATAR CHAIN!"** Zeke yelled. He ran

over to a large rock that was
tightly stuck into the ground.
He pulled on it to be sure it
wouldn't move under his weight,
but it stayed solid. Zeke lay
on his stomach and hooked
his feet around the rock. He
STRETCHED out in the
direction of the mouth of the
volcano. Then he gestured for
Jez to come over. She lay on
her stomach and Zeke grabbed
her legs firmly. Then he gently
lowered her over the edge of the
volcano mouth.

My turn.

I shimmied down the side of the opening of the volcano, clinging to Jez's body like a rope and slowly descending. When I got to her arms, she grabbed onto my legs and I **FLIPPED** upside down.

I felt my legs **SLIP** slightly in Jez's grasp and I gasped in shock.

"Let's make this quick, OK?" Jez urged.

I reached my arms out as far as I could stretch them, almost touching Gabe, who was still hanging from the rock that jutted out of the wall of the crater.

"Gabe, you've gotta **LET GO** and grab me!" I yelled.

"I—I can't!" he stammered. "It's **TOO RISKY.**"

"Sometimes you have to risk things in life," Zeke called down. "You have no choice!"

Gabe looked **TERRIFIED.**

"Gabe," I said flatly. "You can do this. I've got you. Reach your free arm up and then let go and I'll grab you."

Gabe's eyes were full of fear. But then he frowned and nodded.

"Ready?" he called.

"Ready!" I yelled back.

"Three—two—one—**GO!**"

Gabe swung his free arm upward
and launched his body toward
me, releasing the rock. I saw
him scrunch his eyes tight as
I grabbed his arm in a firm grip.

"GOT YOU!" I told him.

"We've got him!" Jez yelled back
up the chain to Zeke.

"Now climb up us!" I instructed Gabe.

He scurried over our bodies like
a rat along a drainpipe. Once he

was back on firm ground, I did the same. Then Jez. Once we were all back up at the top, we began **LAUGHING** hysterically.

"I can't believe that worked!" Gabe huffed. "Do you know the odds of that actually working?"

But our laughter was interrupted by another rumble. The ground shook more violently than before. Then there was a loud **BANG!**

"Whoa," I gasped, as red spurts of lava **SHOT UP** into the air. "We need to get out of here!"

Smoke started billowing out of the top of the volcano and the earth continued to tremble. I was no volcanologist, but I could tell this thing was **GONNA BLOW!**

WEDNESDAY—
LATER STILL

Zeke **COUGHED.** "How are we gonna stop our lungs from filling with **SMOKE?**"

"Wait!" Gabe screeched, throwing his **BACKPACK** onto the ground. He unzipped it and began rummaging around inside.

"No time for a drink break, Gabe," I said, urging him to get up.

But then he pulled out four large,

black **GAS MASKS**—the kind you saw in movies when the hero went into a toxic wasteland.

"Where on earth did you get these?" Jez asked, shocked.

"ALWAYS PREPARED, right?" Gabe smiled wryly. "My dad works at the chemical plant. I thought I'd bring them along—

you never know when there may be **NOXIOUS GASES** around, right?"

I shook my head. Maybe Gabe's over-preparedness wasn't the worst thing to ever happen to us after all.

We slipped the masks over our heads and could immediately breathe a whole lot better.

"LET'S GO!" I yelled in a muffled voice to my friends.

We ran down from the peak of

the volcano toward the first plateau where the information center was located. There was nobody in sight.

There was another huge **BANG** and we all fell to our knees. Lava shot up into the air above us at the mouth of the volcano.

"Uh, guys," Zeke said. "I think the crater is full."

Sure enough, we could see lava **BUBBLING** out of the top of the volcano and spilling over the sides. Thick trails of oozing, steaming lava began flowing right toward us!

"We've gotta **RUN!**" Jez squealed.

"Mildred said we'd never outrun the lava," Gabe cried.

We were **DOOMED!** If only we could get down the hill faster.

I thought back to how I raced down the hill at school on my lunch tray to rescue Gabe's notebook. If only Gabe had lunch trays in his bag of tricks.

But then I had an **IDEA!**

"I've got it!" I declared, and ran toward the information center.

I burst through the doors and looked around. Mildred had mentioned something about lava-proof material. I saw the

SHEETS OF METAL

hanging on the wall. I grabbed one and pulled down hard. The cables holding it up snapped and I dumped it on the floor. Then I grabbed the other one and did the same.

They were cold and smooth but lighter than I would have thought. I gathered them both up and ran back outside.

"Here!" I yelled. "Two to a sheet!"

"WHOA, SURF'S UP!"

Zeke exclaimed.

"Gabe, come with me. Jez, you go with Zeke," I said.

Gabe sat on the front of the sheet of metal. I positioned it right at the top of the steepest part of the track. Then I bent down and held the metal sheet with both hands. With my feet on the ground, I began to run, pushing the metal sheet in front of me like an athlete beginning a bobsled ride.

As we picked up speed and started hurtling down the mountainside, I jumped onto the back of the sheet and sat behind Gabe as if we were riding a toboggan together.

We **WHIZZED** down the track, leaning left and right to stay on the path as it curved its way down the mountain.

Suddenly there was another huge

BOOM!

I turned to look behind me and saw Zeke and Jez following. But behind them, the lava was now flowing super fast. And it was **GAINING ON US.**

WEDNESDAY—
EVEN LATER

I could hear the **WHOOSHING** of the hot, molten lava streaming behind us. I could smell the smoke and feel the heat of it getting closer to us.

"Here we **GOOOOO!**" Zeke's voice yelled.

"Nooooo!" I cried as I heard the lava catch up to him and Jez. Surely they were goners?!

But then I saw them zooming down next to me, **RIDING** the wave of lava. The metal really *was* lava-proof!

Another **WAVE OF LAVA** came shooting down the mountain and quickly swept up Gabe and me.

"AAAAAAAGGGHH!" Gabe and I screamed as the hot lava wave picked up our sled and sent us **FLYING DOWN** the mountainside.

We couldn't hold on without getting our fingers in the lava, so we had to stand and crouch low, **SURFING** the metal sheet as it surged lower.

I clung onto Gabe, who I didn't think was much of a surfer. And I was quietly thankful for learning to surf with my grandpa at the beach each summer.

As we sped down toward the flat ground, I noticed there was **NO BOAT** at the dock.

"Mr. Rockface left us here!" I yelled. "What do we do now?!"

The lava wave crashed into the ocean, sending us **HURTLING OFF** our metal surfboards into the sea. There was a gigantic **SIZZLING** sound as the hot liquid clashed with the cold ocean, and smoke went billowing up into the sky.

"SWIM!" Jez cried.

We had to get away from the hot lava. Even though it was now in the ocean, that water would turn into a **BOILING** pot in seconds.

I gasped as the ocean waves smacked me in the face. Gabe **SPLUTTERED,** trying to keep up, but it was clear he wasn't the best swimmer. I swam over to him, pulled off his backpack, and flipped him over so his face was looking up toward the sky. Then I tugged him along behind me as I sidestroked my way toward **THE ROCKS** along the other end of the shore.

Jez and Zeke followed.

Once we made it to the rocks, we **HEAVED** our exhausted bodies up on top of them and **COLLAPSED.** We were all breathing heavily.

We looked back at the volcano, which still had smoke billowing out from the top. The lava river had slowed down and continued to crash into the ocean. And it was bleeding into the sea, inching **CLOSER** to us.

"Are we safe here on these rocks?" Gabe panted.

I looked up and saw several new streams of lava coming down from other parts of the volcanic mountainside. It wouldn't be long before it reached us on the rocks. So, we couldn't go back to land—we'd be made into avatar soup. But if we went back into the ocean, we'd drown. And if we stayed here, these rocks would turn into hot plates as soon as the lava touched them.

"Oh no, I can hear another **EXPLOSION** coming!" Jez yelled.

There was indeed a **RUMBLING** noise. But it sounded different from the last explosion.

Then, from over the volcano, we saw a **HELICOPTER**

coming our way. We jumped up
and waved our arms.

"HEEEEELLLP!" we screamed.

The door of the helicopter was
open. And who was hanging out
by a harness and rope?

"MILDRED!" we gasped.

The harness lowered her down until she was with us on the rocks. Then a ladder slowly unfurled. The helicopter was **DEAFENING** above us as it sprayed water all over the place.

"COME ON, avatars!" she called, ushering each one of us up the dangling ladder.

One by one, we climbed the long ladder into the helicopter. Mildred came up last, making sure we were all safe inside.

We **COLLAPSED** into the seats and pulled off our gas masks. We strapped ourselves in as Mildred shut the door, and the helicopter took off back toward land.

"How did you know to come get us?" I asked, **PANTING.**

"I was checking that all the kids were accounted for with

Mr. Rockface. He said nobody had reported their buddy missing. Then I realized those nice young avatars I was talking to earlier weren't there. The buddy system is deeply flawed," she said.

"That's what I said!" Gabe added.

"So I immediately got a rescue operation happening. But how on earth did you **BEAT** the lava down the mountain? And where did you get those gas masks?" Mildred asked in wonder.

"We surfed the metal sheets from

the information center," I said, smiling. "And the masks? Well, luckily we had **GABE** here. He's always prepared."

I patted Gabe on the shoulder and he **BEAMED.**

"Well, let's get you all back home," Mildred said.

I sighed, exhausted, and rested my head on the seat behind me. Gabe leaned his head on my arm, still catching his breath. Then he fell asleep. I didn't mind.

FRIDAY LUNCHTIME

"Nah, bruh, the most **EPIC** part was when you went flying past us on the metal surfboard—I thought you were lava lunch, but you **OWNED IT!**" I hollered, high-fiving Zeke.

Since the field trip, we'd become a little bit **FAMOUS** for escaping the volcano. Even the news did a report on it and we got interviewed! Then we had to go get checked out at the doctor's, but everything was OK, so we were back in school, recounting our **AWESOME** adventure.

Jez took the last bite of her apple then lobbed the core into the nearby trash can. Right next to it was Gabe, who was standing nervously and holding his lunch.

"Gabe, do you want to **JOIN US?**" I asked.

His eyes lit up and he hurriedly sat down. "Thanks, guys!" he said, opening his lunch and starting to eat.

NOM, NOM, NOM!

"You'll never guess what I'm taking up," Gabe said. "Surfing!"

"Wow, that's a bit **RISKY** for you, Gabe," Zeke said, winking at him.

"Yeah, it is. But I had a long talk with my parents. They agreed with me that sometimes you have to take on the risk in order to have some fun. And they were fine with the idea of surfing—as long as it wasn't on **LAVA** again!" Gabe said.

We **LAUGHED** and nodded in understanding.

"Hey, **NERDS,**" a snide voice said from behind us. We turned and saw Trip standing there. "You know what? I don't believe for a second that you surfed down that lava. There's **NO WAY** you are that cool," he sneered.

"BEAT IT, TRIP," Jez said, rolling her eyes.

Trip snarled at her, then **LUNGED OUT** and stole the cap from my head.

"Hey!" I roared as Trip turned to run away with it.

Quick as a flash, Gabe reached into his bag and pulled out a **YO-YO.** He extended it toward Trip so it unfurled on its string. It knocked my cap out of Trip's hand and sent it flying into the air. The cap somersaulted

a few times then landed back on
my head with a plop.

Gabe then shot his yo-yo outward
again, tangling it up in Trip's legs.
Trip wobbled then **TOPPLED
OVER** on the grass, right as
Gabe retracted his yo-yo back
into his palm.

"Ugh, I'll get you!" Trip **HISSED** as he stood up and ran away, embarrassed.

"Whoa, great move, bruh!" Zeke said, fist-bumping Gabe. "Lucky you had that yo-yo, right?"

"You know me," Gabe giggled, **"ALWAYS PREPARED!"**

And we all burst out **LAUGHING.**

ALSO AVAILABLE:

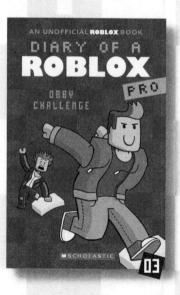

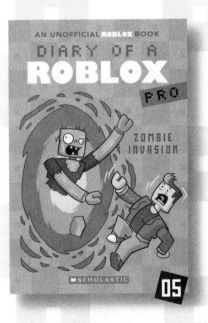